POEM BY
CLEMENT C. MOORE

The Night

To the memory of my mom, Maggi Rogers

Published by
Dial Books for Young Readers
A division of Penguin Young Readers Group
345 Hudson Street
New York, New York 10014

Pictures copyright © 2003 by Jacqueline Rogers
All rights reserved
Designed by Jacqueline Rogers and Nancy R. Leo-Kelly
Text set in Mrs. Eaves
Additional hand-lettering done by the artist
Manufactured in China on acid-free paper
10 9 8 7 6 5 4 3 2 1

Library of Congress Cataloging-in-Publication Data
Moore, Clement Clarke, 1779–1863.
The night before Christmas : a goblin tale /
poem by Clement C. Moore ; pictures by Jacqueline Rogers.
p.   cm.
Summary: An illustrated version of the poem about the annual
visit of Santa, in which all the characters are depicted as goblins.
ISBN 0-8037-2785-2 (acid-free paper)
1. Santa Claus—Juvenile poetry. 2. Christmas—Juvenile poetry.
3. Children's poetry, American.
[1. Santa Claus—Poetry. 2. Christmas—Poetry.
3. American poetry. 4. Narrative poetry.]
I. Rogers, Jacqueline, ill. II. Title.
PS2429.M5 N5 2003   811'.2—dc21 2001008749

The art for this book was painted in acrylics on gessoed paper. Santa was modeled by
my friend Bob Richardson (who even had the whole suit!). The goblins were modeled
by my imagination, although they appear cuter in this book than they do in my head.

Before Christmas

A Goblin Tale

pictures by JACQUELINE ROGERS

Dial Books for Young Readers

'Twas the night before Christmas, when all through the house
Not a creature was stirring, not even a mouse;
The stockings were hung by the chimney with care,
In hopes that St. Nicholas soon would be there;

The children were nestled all snug in their beds,
While visions of sugar-plums danced in their heads;
And Mamma in her kerchief, and I in my cap,
Had just settled our brains for a long winter's nap,

When out on the lawn there arose such a clatter,
I sprang from the bed to see what was the matter.
Away to the window I flew like a flash,
Tore open the shutters and threw up the sash.

The moon on the breast of the new fallen snow
Gave the luster of mid-day to objects below,
When, what to my wondering eyes should appear,
But a miniature sleigh, and eight tiny reindeer,

With a little old driver so lively and quick,
I knew in a moment it must be St. Nick.
More rapid than eagles his coursers they came,
And he whistled, and shouted, and called them by name:

"Now, Dasher! now, Dancer! now, Prancer and Vixen!
On, Comet! on, Cupid! on, Donder and Blitzen!
To the top of the porch! to the top of the wall!
Now dash away! dash away! dash away all!"

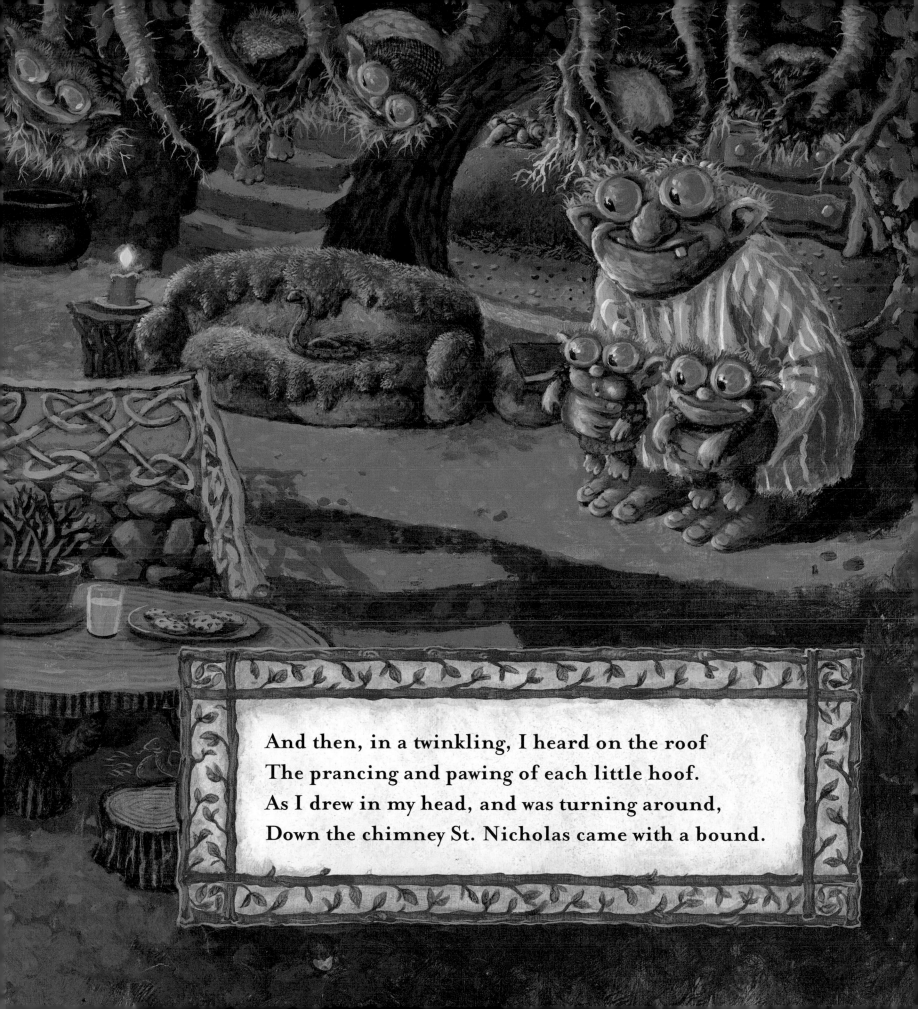

And then, in a twinkling, I heard on the roof
The prancing and pawing of each little hoof.
As I drew in my head, and was turning around,
Down the chimney St. Nicholas came with a bound.

He was dressed all in fur, from his head to his foot,
And his clothes were all tarnished with ashes and soot;
A bundle of toys he had flung on his back,
And he looked like a peddler just opening his pack.

His eyes—how they twinkled! his dimples how merry!
His cheeks were like roses, his nose like a cherry!
His droll little mouth was drawn up like a bow,
And the beard of his chin was as white as the snow;

The stump of his pipe he held tight in his teeth,
And the smoke it encircled his head like a wreath;
He had a broad face and a little round belly,
That shook, when he laughed, like a bowlful of jelly.

He was chubby and plump, a right jolly old elf,
And I laughed when I saw him, in spite of myself;
A wink of his eye and a twist of his head,
Soon gave me to know I had nothing to dread;

He spoke not a word, but went straight to his work,
And filled all the stockings; then turned with a jerk,

And laying his finger aside of his nose,

And giving a nod, up the chimney he rose;

He sprang to his sleigh, to his team gave a whistle,
And away they all flew like the down on a thistle.

But I heard him exclaim ere he drove out of sight,

"Happy Christmas to all, and to all a good night."